EGMONT

We bring stories to life

First published in Great Britain in 2007 by Dean,
an imprint of Egmont UK Limited
239 Kensington High Street, London W8 6SA

Thomas the Tank Engine & Friends™

A BRITT ALLCROFT COMPANY PRODUCTION

Based on The Railway Series by The Reverend W Awdry
Photographs © 2007 Gullane (Thomas) LLC. A HIT Entertainment Company

Thomas the Tank Engine & Friends and Thomas & Friends are trademarks of Gullane (Thomas) Limited.
Thomas the Tank Engine & Friends and Design is Reg. US. Pat. & Tm. Off.

HiT entertainment

ISBN 978 0 6035 6234 1
7 9 10 8 6
Printed in Singapore

Gordon and Spencer

The Thomas TV Series

DEAN

The Fat Controller's engines like doing special jobs for him. It makes them feel really useful and important!

One day, Gordon heard some exciting news. He chuffed up next to Thomas, who was waiting for his turn at the wash down.

"Move aside!" Gordon huffed. "This is a special day and I need to look my best!"

"Why is it a special day?" Thomas asked.

"The Duke and Duchess are visiting the Island," boasted Gordon. "The Fat Controller is sure to ask me to show them around. I am the fastest engine on the Island!"

After Gordon had been washed and polished, he rushed off to meet the Duke and Duchess.

Gordon was speeding happily towards Knapford Station when the signals turned red! Gordon was moved to a siding.

"What's going on?" puffed Gordon, crossly.

Suddenly there was a loud whoosh and a sharp whistle. A big silver engine rocketed past!

"Steaming pistons!" cried Gordon. "Who was that?"

When Gordon arrived at Knapford Station, he saw the sleek silver engine having a wash down and talking to James.

"Who are you?" Gordon asked.

"This is Spencer," James chuffed. "He's the fastest engine in the world!"

"I'm the Duke and Duchess's private engine," boasted Spencer. "I take them everywhere."

Gordon was very disappointed. He wouldn't be able to show the Duke and Duchess around the Island.

The Fat Controller came to see the engines. "There will be a reception this afternoon for the Duke and Duchess at Maron Station," he said.

"That's the other side of Gordon's Hill," James told Spencer.

"You'll need to take on plenty of extra water," said Gordon, helpfully.

"I have plenty of water," wheeshed Spencer. He raced out of the yard with the Duke and Duchess aboard. Gordon felt sad. It wasn't going to be a special day after all.

Spencer showed the Duke and Duchess lots of beautiful places all over the Island. But he never stopped once to take on water.

Gordon had some passengers to unload at Wellsworth Station. He was feeling more miserable than ever.

"Make way!" boomed Spencer, racing past on his way to the reception.

"Big shiny show off!" Thomas snorted.

"Don't forget water!" shouted Gordon. But Spencer didn't listen.

When Spencer reached Gordon's Hill, he began
to struggle. The hill grew steeper and steeper.
And Spencer went slower and slower.

He puffed! He panted! He pulled with all his strength.
But it was no use.

Spencer had run out of steam!

Spencer's Driver called The Fat Controller for help.
"I'll send one of my engines immediately," he promised.

The Stationmaster went to find Gordon. "The Fat
Controller has an important job for you," he said.
"An engine is stuck on a hill."

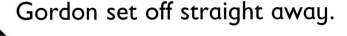 Gordon set off straight away.

Gordon was surprised to see Spencer stuck on the line! "What's wrong?" he asked.

"No water," Spencer snapped. "I must have a leaky tank."

"Perhaps," smiled Gordon. "But we'd better hurry. Everyone is waiting."

Gordon was soon coupled to Spencer, and they set off.

Gordon felt very proud as he pulled Spencer and his coaches into Maron Station. Spencer felt embarrassed!

"Well done, Gordon," said The Fat Controller. "You are a Very Useful Engine!"

They were just in time for the start of the grand reception!

"So, what do you think of Spencer now?"
Thomas whispered to James.

"Too much puff and not enough steam!"
laughed James.

"What about you, Gordon?" Thomas asked.

But Gordon just smiled. It had
turned out to be a special day,
after all!